First published in Farsi in 1968 by Kanoun Parvaresh Fekri, Tehran, Iran

First published in the United Kingdom in 2015 by Tiny Owl Publishing Ltd

This edition first published in the United States in 2019 by Tiny Owl Publishing Ltd

www.tinyowl.co.uk

Translated by Azita Rassi

© 2015 Tiny Owl Publishing Ltd

Illustrations © Nazar Publisher, Tehran, Iran

A CIP record for this book is available from the Library of Congress.

ISBN 978-1-910328-00-2

The Little Black Fish

Samad Behrangi

Illustrated by Farshid Mesghali

TINY OWL

As the nights grew longer and the year turned toward winter once more, an old fish settled down to tell a story. She was telling the story to her twelve thousand grandchildren fishes. It was an exciting story full of danger as well as sadness, but it was a story that also carried wisdom. The old fish wanted her grandchildren to learn from Little Black Fish's story without having to go into the dangers and sadness of life themselves. This is the story grandmother fish told.

There was once a Little Black Fish who lived with his mother in a stream between one waterfall and another. The stream changed with the weather, but otherwise it was much the same day after day: running water, and other fish, all swimming up and down and around. They weren't very nice or very smart fish.

"Not you again!" they said as they met each other again and again and again.

"Well, who did you expect to meet? You're not likely to meet anybody new here, are you?"

At night the stream went dark, except when the moon was bright in the sky. Little Black Fish saw flickers of moonlight through the thick moss roof of the stone house he shared with his mother. He longed to go out into the nighttime stream to see the moon properly.

The moon in the sky must see so much, thought Little Black Fish. She must be able to see what is beyond our stream. Little Black Fish tried to push the moss away so that he could talk to the moon, and ask questions, but...

"Put that moss back!" said his mother. "Don't go out into the night and get killed, my child. Of all the ten thousand eggs I've laid, you're the only one to hatch and survive. I'm not letting any harm come to you!"

So Little Black Fish just had to wonder what might be beyond the stream, because it seemed that he would never be able to find out.

Little Black Fish was thinking so much about where the water that flowed into their stream came from, and where it flowed out to, that he wasn't swimming properly alongside his mother on their daily swims up and down and around.

"Keep up!" said his mother. "What's the matter with you, child? Come on, we must swim up and down and around, just as the other fishes do or they'll start to think that there's something wrong with us. We don't want to be different."

There *was* something different about Little Black Fish. He ached with longing to go beyond the stream, and to discover for himself what might be there.

One night he couldn't sleep for wondering. So, the next morning, he said to his mother, "I have decided something, but you won't like it."

"Then don't tell it to me!" said his mother. "You silly child! Come along and swim with the others before they think that you are odd."

"But I am not going to swim with them, or with you, any more," said Little Black Fish. "I must swim beyond the stream, and explore. I want to see if the stream goes on and on, or whether it comes to an end. Don't you want to know that too?"

"No I don't!" said his mother. "I might have when I was young like you, but I learned sense as I grew up, and you must too. The stream just flows and *is*, that's all, and that's enough. We don't need to know any more than that."

"But it must flow to somewhere," said Little Black Fish. "And it must come to an end, mustn't it? Just as days end, and nights end, and years end, and..."

"Oh, that's silly talk!" said his mother. "Come on, it's time to swim up and down and around, and forget all your nonsense." But "No," said Little Black Fish. "I don't want to spend my life swimming up and down and around, and then grumbling that there isn't anything more to life. Perhaps there is more to life, and perhaps the world *is* more than our stream!"

"Our stream is the world!" said his mother.

Just then one of the neighboring fish came to see what they were arguing about.

"It's time to swim up and down and around," said the nosy neighbor fish. "Are you having trouble with your child, Neighbor?"

"I am!" said Little Black Fish's mother. "The silly child wants to swim beyond the stream, to see the world."

The nosy neighbor turned to Little Black Fish. "What makes you think that you know more than your mother, when she has lived in the world so much longer than you?"

That made Little Black Fish angry. "I know that I am bored of swimming up and down and around. I know that I don't want to end up as a moany old fish like you!"

"Disgraceful!" shouted the nosy neighbor fish.

"I am sorry," said Little Black Fish's mother. "Somebody wicked must have put these ideas into his head."

"No they didn't!" said Little Black Fish. "I have eyes to see and a brain to think. I have my own ideas!"

"It must have been that twisty little snail who made him think this way," said the nosy neighbor.

"Oh, that snail was certainly a bad influence," said Little Black Fish's mother. "I never did trust him. He wasn't one of us."

"He was my friend!" said Little Black Fish.

"Fishes have no business being friends with snails," said his mother.

"And they have no business being *enemies* with snails either!" said Little Black Fish. "But you killed him! You killed my friend!"

"Well, that's all in the past now," said the nosy neighbor. "And it was just as well, considering the things he said."

"He only said the same things that I say now," said Little Black Fish. "So are you going to kill me too?"

Their arguing had attracted many more nosy fish from the stream to come and see what the fuss was about. They all had opinions to offer.

"That child should be made to do as his elders and betters tell him to!"

"He should be punished!"

But now Little Black Fish's mother was getting scared. "Don't you hurt my child!"

"Well, if you can't bring him up to be a proper fish, what do you expect?" asked another. "I'm ashamed to be living near you!"

That's when Little Black Fish's friends came to the rescue. While the moany old fishes talked nastily about Little Black Fish and his mother, Little Black Fish's friends swum to surround him, and they swam him away from the crowd.

"If you go, Little Black Fish, we won't want you back!" shouted a nasty old fish.

"Oh, what can I do?" cried Little Black Fish's mother.

"Don't cry for me, Mother!" called Little Black Fish. "I am happy to go, and maybe I will return one day and tell you all what I found!"

Little Black Fish's friends went with him to the waterfall at the end of their stream.

"Thank you," said Little Black Fish. "Don't forget me when I'm gone."

"How could we forget you?" said his friends. "You are being brave in order to find out more. We admire you!"

"Goodbye!"

Little Black Fish slid down the waterfall—wheee!—to fall into a deep still pool, quite different from the stream he had just left.

There were thousands of small black tadpoles in that still water, and they had never seen a fish before.

"Ha ha!" they laughed. "Look at that thing! He's not like us, he's strange!"

"Don't be unkind to me," said Little Black Fish. "Let me introduce myself. My name is Little Black Fish. What are your names?"

"Tadpole."

"Tadpole."

"Tadpole," they all said.

"Are you *all* called Tadpole?" said Little Black Fish.

"Of course," said one tadpole. "We are all the finest sort of tadpoles."

"And the prettiest. Not like you!"

Little Black Fish laughed. "How can you know that you are fine and pretty when you've never met anybody else? Don't you know that there are other creatures who also think they are the finest and the prettiest? You're all wrong!"

"No, *you're* the one who is wrong!" said the tadpoles. "We swim around the world all day long, but there are only our parents and us, oh, and some teeny-weeny worms that don't count anyway."

"You don't go around the world, you know. You just go around this pool," said Little Black Fish.

"But this pool *is* the world," said the tadpoles.

"Don't you wonder where your waterfall comes from?" asked Little Black Fish. "It comes from a place outside your pool. It comes from the place where I lived, and that place is different from this pool."

"You're silly!" said the tadpoles. "We don't believe you!"

Oh well, thought Little Black Fish. Some creatures just like to stay ignorant. But perhaps they get wise when they get older? So Little Black Fish asked the tadpoles, "Where is your mother?"

"Here I am," said a gruff voice behind Little Black Fish, making him start with a splash.

The frog was sitting on a rock by the pool. "What do you want?" she asked. "I heard what you were telling my children, and you've no right to make up stories about other places. I've lived in this pool all my life, and I know that there's no world beyond it. You're trying to trick my children into following you!"

"Oh, honestly!" said the frustrated Little Black Fish. "Even if you live a hundred times as long as you already have, you'll stay as ignorant as you are!" Which was a rude thing to say to the frog, but Little Black Fish had had enough of being told off for one day.

The big frog leaped into the water toward Little Black Fish, but flick–flick went Little Black Fish's tail, and off he shot, disturbing the mud and worms at the bottom of the pool as he made his escape.

If Little Black Fish had been able to look down on the valley as the moon did each night, he would have seen that it was a valley with as many bends as those wriggly worms. He would have seen that the stream became bigger and fuller and wider the farther along the valley it traveled. It glinted like silver string when the moon shone down, and that silver string forked off into two different directions at a place where a big rock sat in the water.

But it was still daytime now. In the hot sunshine a lizard as big as a big man's hand lay on a rock, basking in the warmth and watching a crab on the sand eating a frog. The lizard spotted something small and black in the water. It was Little Black Fish.

Little Black Fish was also watching something. He was watching the crab, which was a creature of a kind he'd never seen before. It had big pincers, and it scuttled sideways when it moved. Truly the world beyond the stream was full of surprises!

"Hello, strange creature!" said Little Black Fish.

"I'm a crab," said the crab. "Do come closer, little one, and then you can see me properly. Come on!"

"Ha! You don't catch me that easily!" said Little Black Fish. "I am going to see the world and I don't want to be eaten by you, sir, before I've seen it all!"

"Are you scared of me?" asked the crab in a mocking voice. "Poor baby!"

"I just use my eyes and brain to work out what your game is," said Little Black Fish. "I don't need to prove my bravery to you, and I can see exactly what you're doing to that poor frog!"

The crab smiled. "Oh, I'm only eating the frog because I don't like having frogs around the place. They are arrogant and think that the world belongs to them. It doesn't. So I'm tidying things up, you see. You have nothing to worry about because you aren't a frog. Come close. Come!"

As he spoke, the crab was scuttling over to get nearer to Little Black Fish. Little Black Fish thought that his sideways scuttling looked funny, and he was laughing as he backed away from those pincers coming nearer.

"You can't..." began Little Black Fish. But before he could finish what he was about to say, a huge black shadow fell over the water, and something— bonk!—knocked the crab deep into the sand.

"What—?" began Little Black Fish. He looked up to see more new creatures. There was a shepherd boy with goats and sheep, and one of the goats had butted the crab into the sand as it put its head down to drink.

Little Black Fish watched in amazement, and listened to the strange bleating sounds that he'd never ever heard before. The world had so many new things to show him. How many more new things might he find before he found the end of the stream?

The lizard had been laughing at the crab's struggle to get out of the sand. So Little Black Fish asked the lizard, "Dear lizard, I am on my way to find the end of the stream. You sit there and see what goes on in the world. Is there any advice that you can give me?"

"Well," said the lizard. "You must look out for pelicans. And if you get as far as the sea, you must look out for swordfish and seabirds."

"What are pelicans?" asked Little Black Fish.

"They are big birds, and tricky birds!" said the lizard. "Pelicans have pouches that hang from their big beaks. They swim in the water, and catch fish in those pouches. If they are hungry, they swallow the fishes into their stomachs."

"What if they aren't hungry?" asked Little Black Fish hopefully.

"Then they keep the fish in their pouches until they are hungry," said the lizard.

"Oh," said Little Black Fish. "I don't think I want to meet one of them."

"I can give you a knife that will let you cut your way out of a pouch, if you like?" said the lizard.

"Oh, yes please!" said Little Black Fish.

The lizard crawled into the crack in the rock and returned with a very tiny knife made from a thorn.

"Thank you!" said Little Black Fish. "Do you give knives to all the fish you meet?"

"Just to the smart ones who ask the right questions," said the lizard. "Lots of fish have escaped the pouches of pelicans thanks to me. And now those fish work together to escape from the fishermen too."

"How do they do that?" asked Little Black Fish.

"By working together" laughed the lizard. "One fish alone could never escape. But hundreds, all working together, can drag a fisherman's net to the bottom of the sea where they can do no harm." Then the lizard put her ear to the crack of the rock. "Ah, my children have woken up. I must go!" And she disappeared into the crack.

So Little Black Fish set off once more, swimming and thinking. Could the stream really go all the way to what they called the sea, a place with swordfish and seabirds?

There were so many new things to see along the way that
Little Black Fish didn't have time to worry about pelicans and
swordfish and seabirds for long. It was such fun—whee! Splash!—
falling down waterfalls, diving down into the depths before
wiggling upward to start swimming again. Little Black Fish felt the
sun's warmth on his back, and he ate and felt himself getting bigger
and stronger all the time.

That was just as well because the more Little Black Fish found out
about the world, the more he realized that it was a dangerous as well
as a beautiful place.

At one spot, a beautiful doe was drinking water from the stream.
Little Black Fish wanted to talk to the doe and find out about the land
world.

"Hello," he said. "Pretty doe, will you talk to me?"

"A hunter is chasing me," said the doe. "I must hurry
away. He has already shot me once."

And the doe limped away, so Little Black
Fish knew that was true, and he felt sad.

As he swam on down the stream, Little Black Fish saw turtles napping in the warmth of the sun. He heard the laughter of little quail birds echoing in the valley. The wonderful smells of mountain herbs came and went in the air and water. The world could be cruel, but it could be wonderful too.

The farther downstream Little Black Fish swam, the wider and wider the stream became. It gushed through woodlands, where the sunlight dappled through tree branches. Little Black Fish was enjoying swimming. He hadn't met any other fish since he had left his home stretch of stream, but now he was suddenly surrounded by tiny fish.

"Are you new around here?" they asked.

"Yes," said Little Black Fish. "I've come from far away upstream."

"Where are you going to?" asked the tiny fish.

"I'm going to find the end of the stream," said Little Black Fish.

"Which stream?" asked the tiny fish.

"This one that we're swimming in," answered Little Black Fish.

"Oh! We call this the river," said the tiny fish. "Do you know that you will meet a pelican if you keep going down the river?"

"I have heard of pelicans," said Little Black Fish.

Another tiny fish asked, "And do you know what a huge pouch the pelican has, and what he does with it?"

"I have been told about that too," said Little Black Fish, and he felt with his fin that he still had the thorn knife with him, and was glad of it.

"Why do you go toward the pelican, and danger?" asked the same tiny fish.

"I want to know what is at the end of the stream, so I have to take risks and be brave," said Little Black Fish.

When they heard that, some of the tiny fish wanted to go to the end of their river with Little Black Fish, but their parents wouldn't let them.

They told Little Black Fish, "If it wasn't for the danger of the pelican's pouch we would come with you, but the danger is too great, and we are scared."

Beside the river there was a village, and Little Black Fish saw lots of people.

He watched the women and girls of the village come and wash dishes and clothes in the river. Little Black Fish listened to their chatter, and he watched children splashing and laughing in the shallows. It was all very interesting, but it wasn't the end of the stream, so he must be brave and travel onward.

Little Black Fish swam and swam until night came, when he settled to sleep under a rock.

But in the middle of the night Little Black Fish woke up. He saw moonlight on the water, lighting everywhere with a mysterious silvery light. It was beautiful, and this time Little Black Fish could talk to the moon as he'd so longed to do.

"Hello, pretty moon," he said, and the moon replied, "Hello, Little Black Fish. You are a long way from home."

"Yes," said Little Black Fish. "I am seeing the world."

Moon smiled. "The world is huge. From down there you can't see it all as I can."

"I am happy just to see more of the stream," said Little Black Fish. "I just want to see it to the end." He was about to ask the moon how the world looked from so far away, but a cloud began to slide over the moon, shadowing the lovely light.

"Don't go, Moon! Oh, I wish you could light the world all the time," called Little Black Fish.

The sliver of moon still visible in the sky smiled. "My dear little fish, I don't actually have any light of my own. I simply shine light from the sun down onto the Earth."

"I would love to visit you," said Little Black Fish.

"Humans have visited me," said the moon. "Perhaps one day fish will come to me too. Who knows what might be possible?" Little Black Fish wanted to know more, but the dark cloud had finally covered the moon, and she was gone.

Little Black Fish was woken early the next morning by a whisper-chattering of tiny fish. When they saw that Little Black Fish was awake, the tiny fishes all said, "Good morning, Big Black Fish!" To them, Little Black Fish was big!

"You followed me after all!" said Little Black Fish.

"We did," said one of the tiny fish. "But we are still scared. We really don't want to meet a pelican but we *do* want to see the world."

"If you worry too much about dangers, you will never do anything interesting," said Little Black Fish. "And the world is s—"

But before he could finish what he was saying, the watery world went suddenly dark. Something came up from under them, and something else from above, and they were trapped.

"A pelican has us in his pouch!" said Little Black Fish. "But don't worry, little friends, because I know a way to escape."

The tiny fish were crying. They weren't listening properly to what Little Black Fish had said. One of them told him, "You tricked us, Big Black Fish! Now the pelican will swallow us all, and we will die!"

Their dark pouch-prison shook, and a scary chuckle echoed in the pouch water. The pelican was laughing. He said, "You poor little teeny-tiny fish who are hardly big enough to make a meal! Shall I swallow you all, or shall I take pity and spare one or two of you to swim another day, eh? Hahaha..." He thought it was all a great joke, but it wasn't funny for the fishes. The tiny fish were desperate. They pleaded with the pelican, "Oh, Your Highness, Sir Pelican, we know that you are great and good and kind. If you could kindly open your noble beak just a little bit to let us tiny fish out, then you can keep the Big Black Fish for your dinner. And we can tell all we meet what a noble, kind bird you are!"

Another of the tiny fish said, "Oh, Sir Pelican, we were only in your waters because the Big Black Fish tricked us. Please forgive us for trespassing."

"I didn't trick you!" said Little Black Fish to the tiny ones. "Do you think that you can save yourselves by getting me killed?"

That is exactly what they thought.

"Haha!" said the pelican. "Yes, tiny fish, I *will* forgive you, but on one condition."

"Name your condition, Your Highness!" said the tiny fishes.

"Kill the black fish yourselves, and then I shall grant you your freedom!" said the pelican.

"No!" said Little Black Fish. He told the tiny fish, "Don't listen to that cunning bird who wants to set us against each other. I have a plan which can save us all."

But the foolish tiny fish were too scared to listen to Little Black Fish, and, together, they moved toward him, to attack.

"We can save ourselves by killing you!" said the tiny fishes.

"No you can't!" said Little Black Fish. "The pelican won't *ever* let you go. I'll prove it to you."

"How?" said the tiny fishes.

"Like this," said Little Black Fish. "I will play dead, as if you *have* killed me. And then we shall see if the pelican releases you or not. If the pelican isn't true to his word, then I will release you myself with my knife." Little Black Fish took out his thorn knife to show that he could do what he said he would.

"All right then," said the tiny fishes. "We'll pretend to fight you, and then you pretend to be dead."

So that's what they did, and when Little Black Fish lay still in the bottom of the pelican's pouch, the tiny fishes said, "Oh, Your Highness, Sir Pelican, we've killed Big Black Fish, just as you wanted."

"Haha!" said the pelican. "Well done, tiny fish. As your reward I will swallow you all alive so that you can enjoy a good tour of my belly!"

And in the blink of an eye those tiny fish were gulped down the pelican's throat.

So Little Black Fish lifted up his knife, and he cut open that nasty lying pelican's pouch and, with a flick-flick of his tail, away he swam through the hole in the pouch, off into the river once more.

Little Black Fish swam and swam until there was no valley, no mountains, and the river flowed widely over a flat plain. Small streams joined the river from left and right, bringing more and more water. So this river is the end of lots of streams, thought Little Black Fish in wonder.

With so much water to swim in, Little Black Fish no longer had to swim around rocks, or be careful not to swim into the bank. He could swim wherever he liked! But suddenly—BAM!—Little Black Fish was being attacked by a big thin fish with a mouth in the shape of a double-edged saw. It was the swordfish he had heard about, and in this great wide river there was nowhere to hide!

Little Black Fish dived downward, and flicked side to side, trying to get away from those terrifying teeth. He swam down into the depths of the river, where he came across a shoal of thousands and thousands of fish.

"Please help me!" said Little Black Fish to one of the fishes in the shoal. "I've come from far away, and now I've escaped from the swordfish. But where am I?"

The fish spoke over his shoulder to the other fishes. "Look!" he said. "Here's another one asking the same question that they all do." Then he said to Little Black Fish, "This, my friend, is the sea."

"The sea!" said Little Black Fish in wonder.

"Yes," said the fish. "It is where all streams and rivers end. Are you going to join our shoal? You'd be very welcome."

"Thank you," said Little Black Fish. "I think that I'll just swim around on my own a bit first. I want to explore the sea. And then I will join your shoal. I would like to work with you to drag down a fisherman's net!"

"Enjoy your swim," said the fish. "But if you swim to the surface, be sure to stay clear of the seabird. She likes to catch four or five fishes every day, and if you're not careful you'll be one of them!"

Little Black Fish swam in the
sea on his own. He could feel
the power of the sea as he
swam, and he saw the bottoms
of boats and seaweed and shells.
The glint of sunlight bouncing on
the surface lured him up to the warm
surface of the sea. He swam happily, thinking,
"Even if I died right now, I have seen the stream to its
end, and I know how it turns into sea. I must try
and return to tell my friends all that I now know."

But Little Black Fish's thoughts were brought to
a shocking end as the seabird swooped and snatched
him from the sea. Little Black Fish wriggled in the seabird's
beak, but he couldn't escape, and he was suffocating in the air as
the seabird flew him away from the water.

I wish she would swallow me quickly, thought Little Black Fish.
At least I could breath for a while in the water in her stomach.

"Quickly, seabird!" gasped Little Black Fish. "I am the sort of fish who turns to poison once I die, so swallow me alive, now!"

The seabird said nothing because she thought that Little Black Fish was tricking her into talking and opening her beak.

Little Black Fish could see that the sea under them was about to turn into land. If the seabird dropped him onto land, he could never survive, so he said, "I will die in your beak before you reach your chicks, and then you will be offering them poison!" gasped Little Black Fish. "Save your children by swallowing me yourself now."

Little Black Fish's body became limp and still, and the seabird began to worry that he was already dead, so that he would poison her if she ate him.

"Little Black Fish, are you still breathing?" she asked. And, of course, speaking meant that she opened her beak! Out jumped Little Black Fish, and he fell through the air, with the seabird diving after him, to fall—splash!—into wonderful reviving seawater in which he could breathe again...only for the seabird to catch him up in her beak once more! And this time she did swallow him whole, down into her dark, damp stomach.

Little Black Fish was not alone in that dark stomach. A very tiny little fish was curled in a corner, crying.

"Don't be so frightened, little one," said Little Black Fish. "Try to be a brave fish, and we will think what we can do to get out of here."

"How can we possibly escape?" said the tiny fish.

"I may not be able to save myself, but I can save you," said Little Black Fish. "And I can save other fish too, by killing the seabird so that she doesn't ever kill fish again."

"But how?" said the tiny fish again. He wasn't crying now.

Little Black Fish held up his thorn knife. "I will cut the seabird from inside," he said. "But first I must save you, tiny fish. I am going to wriggle to tickle the seabird's stomach with my tail. She will want to laugh, and that means she will open her beak. You must be ready to jump out as soon as her beak opens."

"But what about you?" asked the tiny fish.

"Don't you worry about me. You just swim for your life, back to the shoal where you can be safe," said Little Black Fish.

Then Little Black Fish started to wriggle this way and that, fluttering his tail to tickle the seabird's belly. The tiny fish was ready, and as soon as the seabird opened her beak to laugh, the tiny fish jumped out of her mouth and escaped.

The tiny fish waited in the water for a while, hoping to see Little Black Fish escape too, but that didn't happen.

What did happen was that the seabird suddenly flapped with terror and pain, and then she died, falling into the water. But the Little Black Fish was never seen again.

And that was the end of the grandmother fish's story.

"It's bedtime now," she told her twelve thousand grandchildren.

"But you didn't tell us what happened to the tiny fish who was saved by Little Black Fish!" said the children.

"That's a story for another night," said their grandmother. "Goodnight!"

Eleven thousand, nine hundred and ninety-nine little fishes said goodnight and went straight to sleep. Grandmother fish fell asleep too. But one little red fish couldn't sleep for thinking about that story. All night she thought of how the stream turned into a river and then into sea, and all the wonderful things you could meet along the way...

A note from the publisher

This book was my favorite when I was a child growing up in Iran. It was first published in 1968 and was actually banned—can you believe that? It's now considered a children's classic in Iran and in many other parts of the world. What makes it so special? And why is it relevant today? There are still many countries where people don't want to see what's beyond their borders—like the little fish who swim around and around, not daring to see the wonders of the rest of the world. But Little Black Fish dares to see the world beyond his stream. Can you imagine what it was like for Little Black Fish seeing new creatures and places for the first time?

This story about a fish daring to mix with other kinds of creatures and other ways of life offers an opportunity to discuss the big questions at the heart of political debate.

Delaram Ghanimifard, Publisher

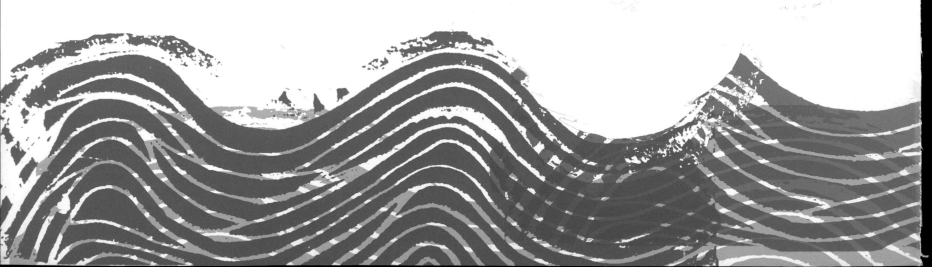

About the Author and Illustrator

Samad Behrangi was one of Iran's most influential authors and teachers. He was also a folklorist, translator, and social critic. Many of his books encouraged people to change their lives for the better. His tragically early death in 1967, rumored to have been ordered by the Iranian government, has given him a legendary status.

Farshid Mesghali created the striking mixed-media illustrations for *The Little Black Fish*. In 1968, he won the highest graphic award at the Bologna Children's Book Fair, and the Honorary Diploma of the Bratislava Biennial Book Fair. In 1974, Farshid Mesghali won the Hans Christian Andersen award for illustration, one of the most famous awards for children's books.

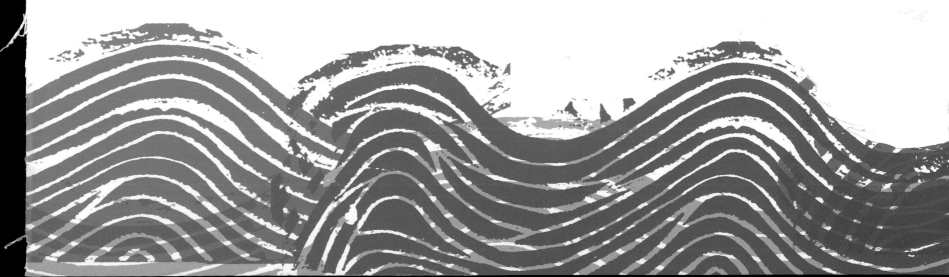